Illustrated by McKenzie Rose West | Written by Jenny Phillips

BOOK 2

Written by Jenny Phillips
Illustrated by McKenzie Rose West
Cover Design by Elle Staples

goodandbeautiful.com

CHAPTER 1

The cold breath of winter hung over the valley. The treehouses were closed for the season, and the woods were still and silent.

Inside Ella's home, however, all was bright and warm. Ella had invited Jake and the two Ts—Thomas and Tori—over to make plans for two new treehouses to be built in the woods behind their homes—a place they now called Treehouse Town.

The children climbed to the attic and began their meeting.

"Well," started Ella. "We have a schoolhouse, a bakery, and a flowershop treehouse. What two types of treehouses should we build next?"

"What about a post office?" suggested Tori.

"Oh!" cried Jake. "I love that idea."

"Me too!" said Ella and Thomas.

"I also like the idea of an art museum," said Ella. "We could create the art ourselves."

"Yes!" said Tori as the

others nodded in agreement.

"Great! Let's get to work making our plans," said Ella.

The four friends sat at a big wooden table and began sketching ideas.

After half an hour, Jake asked for more paper.

"I wonder if there is more up here," Ella said as she started looking through some drawers in an old cabinet.

"Look at this!" cried Ella, pulling out a small, old-looking metal box from the bottom of a large drawer.

"It was hidden under an old quilt," said Ella. "It says Charles Miller on it. That's my great-grandfather's name!"

"What's in it?" asked Jake.

"I don't know. It's locked," said Ella. "Let's show my dad."

When the children got downstairs, they saw so many huge flakes of snow falling outside the window, it looked almost completely white.

Ella's dad had just started a blazing, cozy fire. "Well," he said, "I think we are in for quite a storm. The snow just started fifteen minutes ago,

and it has already covered everything."

Ella's dad frowned and

looked at the group of children.

"I don't think you'll be going home anytime soon. It's a real blizzard out there."

The children looked at each other with smiles as Ella's dad said, "I already phoned your parents and told them we'd keep you until it's safe to go home."

CHAPTER 2

Once the chatter died down about the blizzard, Ella held out the metal box.

"Look Dad! I found this in the attic. It has your grandfather's name on it!"

Within a few minutes, it was discovered that Ella's dad knew nothing about the box, no one had a key, and a screwdriver would not pry it open. Then Ella's white cat, with its gold bell, jumped up onto the windowsill and began meowing loudly and pawing at the window.

"What in the world is she doing?" asked Ella.

They all went to the window but could not see a thing outside, not even the barn— snowflakes filled the sky.

The cat jumped down from the windowsill and went to the front door. The children then heard scratching, barking, and whining coming from the front door.

"Dad! Open it," said Ella, feeling excited and scared at the same time.

Dad cracked the door open

and peered out, and then he opened the door wide. In limped a very wet, very cold little dog that no one knew.

"He's shivering!" cried Tori.

"He's lost!" cried Jake.

"He's cold," said Ella's dad. "Grab a wool blanket, Ella."

Ella's dad led the little dog to the fireplace and wrapped him in the blanket that Ella had brought.

"This is strange," he said. "Besides all of us, there is no one else that lives within miles of here. How could this little dog have gotten here?"

This dog was a mystery.

Ella's mom came in with some food for the dog, but as soon as the dog seemed to have warmed up a bit, it jumped up, ran to the front door, and barked. It then looked at Ella's dad with pleading eyes, ran to his feet, and ran back to the door and barked.

"He's trying to tell me something." Ella's dad watched the dog continue to go from him to the door. "I think he wants me to follow him outside. Perhaps his owner is stuck out in the snow."

He turned to his wife. "Please go grab two large coils of rope from the garage."

He then put on his snow boots, heavy coat, hat, scarf, and gloves.

"You'll get lost in the blizzard!" cried Ella. "You can't see even three feet ahead of you out there."

"That's what the rope is for. I hope whoever is out there is not too far from the house."

He tied the two coils together and then tied one end around his waist. He was out the door with the dog in a flash.

A world of white swirled around him. The dog seemed to know where he was going, so Ella's dad pressed forward in the snow, following the dog.

CHAPTER 3

Before long, Ella's dad was at the end of the rope. He knew

he could not go any farther without getting lost in the snow, so he called out as loud as he could.

He heard the very faint sound of a car door opening and shutting and a muffled man's voice calling back. Ella's dad kept calling, "Follow the sound of my voice! Follow the sound of my voice!"

Within twenty seconds, an older man with white hair bumped into Ella's dad.

"You are my old high school art teacher, Mr. Woods!" cried Dad. "Hold on to me, and we will follow the rope back to the house."

"You saved my life," said the man as he warmed up by the fireplace. "I had just driven out here to run an errand. I could not see a thing, so I just stopped my car in the middle of the road, and the snow started to bury the car. I was frightened, and I prayed. My dog then scratched and barked at the car door until I let him out. He went for help."

"Wow!" said Jake.

"Dogs are amazing animals," said Mr. Woods.

"You look very tired," said Ella's mom. "And you are not going *anywhere* tonight. Come have some supper, and then you can sleep in our warm guest room."

"You are so kind," said Mr. Woods. "You are an answer to my prayer."

No one could leave that night, and every blanket and pillow in the house was used.

The next morning dawned bright and clear, revealing

a sparkling landscape of ice
and snow like the children
had never seen before.

Ella's dad was able to take
Jake and the two Ts home
on his four-wheeler. He also
got Mr. Woods' car into their
driveway, but the roads—

even though they had been plowed—were still very icy.

"Do you have anywhere urgent to go?" Ella's mom asked.

"No," said Mr. Woods. "My wife died two years ago, and we were never blessed with children. I've been so lonely. That's why I bought Charlie, my dog here."

"Well," said Ella's mom, "we would be very pleased if you stayed until the roads are safe. That may be a few days."

"I would be honored. Thank

you!" said Mr. Woods.

After a big breakfast, Ella brought out the metal box again, and Ella's dad tried to pry it open, but it would not budge.

"Someone get me a bobby pin," said Mr. Woods.

He bent and twisted the bobby pin, asked for the metal box, stuck the bobby pin in the key hole, and worked expertly. Within ten seconds, there was a clicking sound, and the lock was open.

CHAPTER 4

There was a quiet hush in the room as Ella opened the box and pulled out two old books bound in leather.

The first book was a sketchbook, and Ella gasped when she saw the first page. It was a sketch of a treehouse.

"Look!" Ella cried. "It's a sketch of the schoolhouse treehouse that we found and restored last summer."

"I *thought* it was my grandfather who built those treehouses," said Ella's dad, "but I still wonder why he built them. Look at the next page, Ella! It's the bakery treehouse that we restored!"

Mr. Woods and Ella's parents were gathered by Ella. They all gasped when Ella turned the page of the sketchbook.

"It's a grocery store treehouse!" cried Ella. "It's

adorable! We never found that one, though."

"No," said Ella's mom. "How do we even know if your great-grandfather built it?"

"We've got some more exploring to do this spring," said Ella.

Ella flipped through all the pages of the sketchbook, and they discovered four more treehouses: a hospital, a restaurant, a fire station, and a library.

"I can't wait to show this to Jake and the two Ts!" said Ella. "They are going to love this!"

"What is the other book, Ella?" asked Ella's mother.

"It's a journal—it's my great-grandfather's journal!" she replied. "Oh, Dad, can I read it?"

"Of course! Maybe we can read it together as a family."

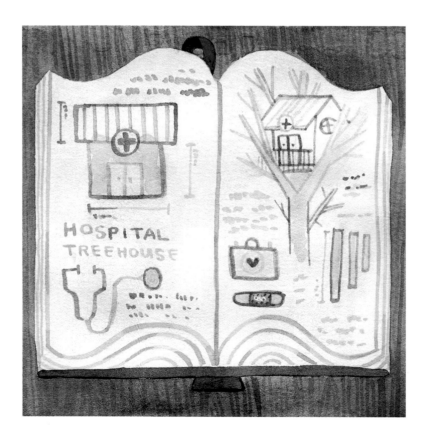

Her dad's smile then faded. "I have some news to share, Ella—some sad news. You know I lost my job eight months ago, and despite my best efforts, I have not been able to find a new job."

"Where did you work?" Mr. Woods asked.

"I worked at home as a Spanish translator. The company I worked for decided not to do any more Spanish products."

He turned to Ella. "We have

not been able to make the payments on our house for four months now. The bank is threatening to take away our home if we miss one more payment."

Ella's mom put her hand on Ella's shoulder. "I have gotten a job at a bakery in the city. I will have to go into the city every day now, and your father is going to come to the city with me each day to look for jobs."

"Oh, Mom!" said Ella as she hugged her mom. "What will I do for school? Who will teach science and math to our homeschool group now? Jake and Tori and Thomas love your lessons."

"Well, I'm not sure," replied Ella's mom. "I need to talk with Jake's and the twins' parents and work something out."

"Did I hear the word *school*?" asked Mr. Woods. "You know I was your father's high school teacher. Boy, would I love to teach this fantastic group of kids!"

Everyone turned toward Mr. Woods with surprised eyes.

"Oh, can he, Mom?" pleaded Ella. She already loved Mr. Woods, with his big smile, his kind face, and the twinkle in his eyes.

"Well, that would be amazing," said Ella's mom, "but I can't let him do that for free."

"Of course you can!" said Mr. Woods. "Your husband saved my life, I have nothing else to do, and it would bring me great joy. You can give me room and board in exchange for my lessons. Your wonderful meals would be payment enough! I'll go home tomorrow and get some clothes and things, and then I'll be ready to start."

Everyone smiled, and Ella's mom happily agreed to the plan.

CHAPTER 5

"Okay!" said Mr. Woods as the homeschool group got started, sitting around the big kitchen table.

"Ella told me about your plans for two new treehouses. Math is an amazing tool for the real world. So after our math lessons each day, we'll use math to plan your treehouses."

For the next three weeks, the children used math to make blueprints of the treehouses and to plan how many nails and how much wood and paint they needed.

In the meantime, Charlie and Ella's cat were becoming good friends, and early

spring was trying its best to melt the snow outside.

Finally, spring had come.
Mr. Woods and the children
looked for the first flowers,

the first tree blossoms,

and the first baby squirrels.

Mr. Woods also helped them open the treehouses that had been shut for winter. He then proposed that they do math in the schoolhouse treehouse and science in the woods, and the children quickly agreed.

They wanted to start building their two new

treehouses, but there was no money for the wood or paint. So, the children explored the woods and found the hospital treehouse that Ella's great-grandfather had built. It had to be restored before

they could use it, but again, they needed money.

Mr. Woods came up with an idea. Early one morning, he and the children went down by the river and collected young willow tree branches.

Mr. Woods taught them all how to create beautiful baskets.

With the permission of their
parents, Mr. Woods drove
the kids to the nearest town

where the children sold the baskets on the street corners.

After five hard days of making and selling baskets, the children had enough money for all the paint, nails, and wood they needed for the treehouses.

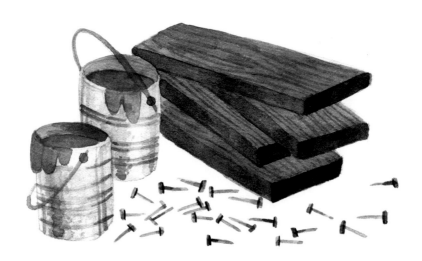

CHAPTER 6

Summer had just arrived when the group finished building the post office treehouse.

Only two weeks later, with the help of Jake's dad and Thomas and Tori's dad, the group finished restoring the

hospital treehouse.

As the group stood back and admired the treehouse, Ella sighed, "Well, we may not get to enjoy it for long. My dad still has not found a job, and the bank is taking our house in thirty days!"

"What!" cried the children.

"We will have to move to an apartment in the city. Some of these treehouses in Treehouse Town won't belong to us anymore."

The group was so sad that everyone stood silent. No one knew what to say.

Ella put on a big smile. "I do have good news, though. My family and I have been reading my great-grandfather's journal every night. We just got to the part where he starts building the treehouses, and you won't *believe* why he did it. I would have never guessed."

"Why did he build them?" asked Tori.

"I'll read it to you," said Ella. "Why don't you all come to my house?" As they were walking in the forest toward Ella's house, Mr. Woods stopped.

"I have an idea for saving your home, Ella!" he nearly shouted. "We are building a museum treehouse next, right?"

Everyone nodded.

"We've got to get that treehouse built as soon as we can," said Mr. Woods. "Let's go listen to your great-grandfather's journal, and then let's start right away on the new treehouse. I have a plan."

"What is your plan?" asked Ella eagerly.

"Well," said Mr. Woods. "I don't think you would believe me if I told you something,

so it will be a surprise. First, let's get back to your house and find out *why* these treehouses were built."

The group walked through the woods, feeling hope as the bees buzzed, the birds sang, and the sun danced between the trees.

CHAPTER 7

Ella sat in the big chair in her living room as she opened her great-grandfather's journal.

"Before I begin," said Ella, "I should tell you that my great-grandfather Charles and his wife married at a young age. After ten years they had not been blessed with children, so Charles had an idea that would allow him to serve children. There used to be an orphanage in the nearby town. Charles built Treehouse Town as a fun, beautiful place for the children to come once a week. I'll read to you what he wrote:

40.

Today was the first day that we opened our treehouse park to the orphanage. I have never seen happier children. For hours they played, going from house to house as they played "Town." They will come every Tuesday now, and it will be my favorite day of the week.

"Wow," whispered Tori after Ella finished reading. "Your great-grandfather was a wonderful man."

"I know," said Ella. "He makes me want to be a better person."

"I wish we could use Treehouse Town to help others," said Thomas. "But I don't know how."

"I agree," said Jake, "but there won't even be a full Treehouse Town if Ella's family loses their home.

Let's get started on the
museum. I can't wait to find
out what Mr. Woods' plan is."

The rest of the day was
spent sawing and nailing.

"We must make this

museum treehouse as big as we can, and we must do it as fast as we can," said Mr. Woods. "At night, you should all work on beautiful art pieces to put in the museum."

That night, the children started some art projects. The next day, they put the roof on the museum treehouse. The morning after that, they all came to start working. Soon after they began, Jake shouted to the rest of the group:

"Come look at this!"

There, on one of the inside walls of the museum, was a small but incredible painting of a deer in a forest. The painting had a gold frame.

"There is no way any of us made *that*," said Tori. "It's one of the most beautiful paintings I have ever seen. How did it get here?"

No one knew, and the children ran like rabbits through the forest to go get Thomas and Tori's dad.

The children and the father

arrived back at the treehouse out of breath, and the children stood quietly as Mr. Lee looked at the painting. He put his head close.

"I don't believe it!" he cried. "This painting is signed by Oliver Orange, the famous artist. This painting must be worth a lot of money. How could it possibly be in this treehouse?" No one knew. They went to ask Mr. Woods, but he was gone, and no one could find him. He returned after Ella went to bed.

The next morning, Ella's parents told her that Mr. Woods was going to need to use the attic for a few weeks, and it was strictly off-limits.

"I'm not sure what is going on," thought Ella, "but I hope this all has to do with saving our home somehow."

CHAPTER 8

Two days later another painting by Oliver Orange appeared in the museum. This painting had a river just like the one that ran through the woods.

"It's beautiful," said Ella.

The kids also worked on their own paintings, and within another week, the treehouse was done. One whole wall was lined with the children's art. They wanted to add sculptures for the middle of the museum, but they had no money for clay.

"Ahh," said Mr. Woods, "there is clay right here in your valley."

Mr. Woods took them to

a place by the river where they found and collected natural clay.

Jake proved to be quite the

artist with clay. He made
some beautiful pots and
painted them bright colors.
The other kids made some
pots, too. When they went
to the treehouse to put their
pots on display, they saw

two more paintings on a wall
that had been empty the day
before. The paintings were
of their very own forest.
They were signed by Oliver
Orange. The children were
baffled!

CHAPTER 9

Ella and her family had continued reading her great-grandfather's journal, and Ella learned about some of the children in the orphanage.

"I wonder if the orphanage building is still there," she said to her mother.

"Me too," said her mother. "We should find out. The

address is in the journal."

So the next day, Ella and her parents drove to the town with the orphanage.

The building was there, but it was no longer an orphanage. A sign stood in front that said "Rescue Refugee Center."

"It's a refugee center now!" said Ella's mom. "We should go in and check it out."

As soon as Ella saw the children inside from different places in the world, she knew what she wanted to do. She told her mom she wanted to invite them to Treehouse Town to get away from their worries, enjoy nature, and have fun.

"We'll see what we can do," said her mom.

The next day, Mr. Woods announced that it was time to earn the money that Ella's family needed to pay the bank for the overdue payments on their home.

He handed Ella the newspaper. "Look at the first page."

Ella took the paper and read the headline:

Oliver Orange to Sell Four Special Paintings at Art Sale in the Woods

"We can't sell those paintings," said Ella. "We don't know who they belong to."

"Yes, we do," said Mr. Woods. "Did you check the back of the paintings?"

The children and parents ran to the treehouse and discovered writing on the back of each painting: *To Ella.*

"They're mine?" said Ella with surprise. "Who gave them to me?"

"I did," said Mr. Woods.

"But where did you get them?" asked Ella.

Mr. Woods smiled. "I painted them."

"But they are signed by Oliver Orange," said Ella's dad.

"Yes," replied Mr. Woods. "Do you know what Oliver Orange looks like?"

"No," replied Ella's dad. "No one knows. Oliver Orange does not want anyone to know who he really is. Everyone knows Oliver Orange is not his real name. It's just his artist's name."

"That's right," said Mr. Woods. "I love to paint, but I don't really want people bothering me just because I am famous."

The group could not believe it. Mr. Woods was a famous painter! They also could not believe the price tags on the paintings.

"Will people buy paintings for *that* much?" asked Jake.

"I think so," replied Mr. Woods.

The next day, fifty cars came down the road to their home for the art sale. Within thirty minutes, all the art was sold, even the children's art!

"Looks like we will all need to create some new art," said Mr. Woods.

"It also looks like we will keep our home!" said Ella's dad. "I cannot thank you enough."

"It's my pleasure," said Mr. Woods. "I have not been this happy in years. I feel almost as if I am a part of your family."

"Oh, you are!" said Ella's mom. "We wish you would stay with us and be 'Grandpa Woods.'"

"That would be my greatest wish, too!" said Mr. Woods.

CHAPTER 10

Grandpa Woods sold his home in the city and moved into the attic at Ella's home. No one could believe that a famous painter would want to live in an attic, but Grandpa Woods did.

"It is perfect!" he said. "I can see the river and the woods from the windows. It inspires my paintings."

The children loved to go up to the attic and watch Grandpa Woods paint.

They also all got to take art lessons from him as part of their homeschool.

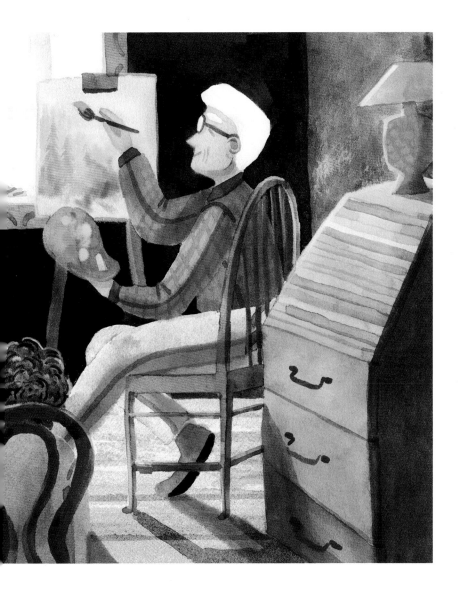

For weeks, the children prepared Treehouse Town for the refugee children.

One day, Charlie the dog helped discover the old grocery store treehouse when he was chasing squirrels.

They worked hard to restore it, and then filled it with shelves, fake food, a cash register, and little shopping carts.

Ella's parents worked with the refugee center to arrange for the children to come to Treehouse Town. Ella's dad was offered a job at the refugee center, and he took it! He got to speak Spanish there, since many of the children were from Cuba. He also helped with many other things. It did not pay very well, but it was enough for their family, and Ella's dad had never enjoyed a job so much.

CHAPTER 11

The last thing to do in Treehouse Town was to make pathways between the treehouses and little toy cars that the children could drive.

Finally, the day arrived. A bus pulled up to Ella's home, and out piled twenty-five excited

children. Within minutes they were running between the treehouses.

The families had prepared a picnic lunch for the children,

and they all ate together in a clearing in the woods.

Ella turned to Grandpa Woods. "This is a dream come true," she said.

"This is not a dream come true," replied Grandpa Woods with a twinkle in his eye. "This is a blessing from God. It started with the kindness of your great-grandfather."

Ella nodded. "It continued with my dad and his courage to save you in the snow, and then your kindness in helping us so we wouldn't have to lose our house."

"It would have never happened," said Grandpa Woods, "without the work and love of all of you children."

"And it definitely would not have happened if it was not for God, who created this beautiful world and watches over us."

"That's right," said Grandpa Woods.

As the evening sun started to set, the bus pulled out,

taking the children back to

the refugee center.

Treehouse Town was once

again still and quiet, waiting

for next Tuesday when the refugee children would come again and fill the woods with laughter.

Try a Level 3 Book from
The Good and the Beautiful Library*

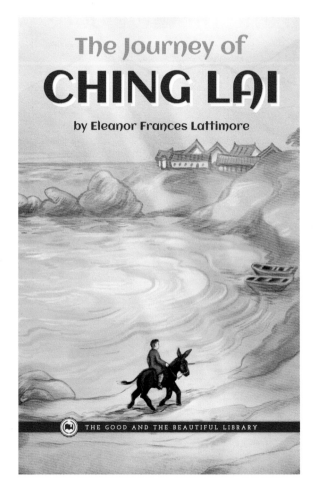

The Journey of
CHING LAI
by Eleanor Frances Lattimore

THE GOOD AND THE BEAUTIFUL LIBRARY

*Reading level assessment is available at
goodandbeautiful.com

Try a Level 3* Book from
The Good and the Beautiful Library

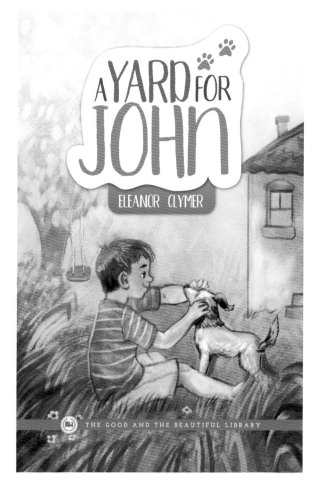

*Reading level assessment is available at
goodandbeautiful.com

Try a Level 3* Book from
The Good and the Beautiful Library

THE GOOD AND THE BEAUTIFUL LIBRARY

May Justus

*Reading level assessment is available at
goodandbeautiful.com*